DATE			

CRANBERRIES

William Jaspersohn

Houghton Mifflin Company   Boston   1991

Acknowledgments

For all their help and cooperation on this project, I wish to thank Cathy Loranger, John Wilson, Jack Crooks, Fred Asmussen, Karen Cornell, Nancy Graca, James Coutu, and Gladys Fischer at Ocean Spray Cranberries, Inc., Lakeville-Middleboro, Massachusetts; that virtuoso jazz pianist Jack Angley, his wife, Dot Angley, and all their crew, especially Brian Sutherland, in Carver, Massachusetts; Wayne Hannula, Scott Hannula, and their splendid crews in South Carver; Marty Feldman, Penny, and all the gang at Light-Works, Burlington, Vermont; and Jeremy, Tom, and Ken at Pro-Cam, White River Junction, Vermont. Blessings, all!

This book is for Terry Adams, Nyomi Armstrong, Jami Beliveau, Kyle Bidwell, Hannah Burbank, Ian Carpenter, Alia Chase, Faith Flynn, Justine Hanlon, Elizabeth Mason Landell, Jennifer Manchester, Matt Peatman, Julie Richards, Jessica Reed, Hannah Smith, Todd Taylor, Christie Wrazen, my son Sam, and the wonderful Sue Waller who taught these children to read and write. I love you all a lot.

—WJ

Library of Congress Cataloging-in-Publication Data

Jaspersohn, William.

    Cranberries / William Jaspersohn.

       p. cm.

    Summary: Depicts the history of cranberries, the stages of cultivation and harvest, and the processing and packaging of this native American fruit.

    ISBN 0-395-52098-3

    1. Cranberries — Juvenile literature.   [1. Cranberries.]

I. Title.

SB383.J37 1991   90-41989

634'.76 — dc20   CIP

                   AC

In June, the cranberry bogs of eastern Massachusetts are in blossom.

The Pilgrims thought the white flowers resembled the heads of birds called cranes. They called the plants "crane-berries," a name later shortened to the one we know today.

Over the weeks, the blossoms drop from the plant, leaving a hard green berry with a brown spike called a style. Earlier, the hollow style carried pollen from the flower to the seeds inside the berry. Before long, the style drops off too. The cranberries grow and grow.

With rain and sunshine, the cranberries grow all summer. In August, they are a waxy green and as big as marbles. In September, their skins begin to redden. In October, when the berries are a bright, rich crimson, they are ripe and ready to be picked.

Cranberries that will be sold fresh or frozen are usually picked by a method called dry harvesting. Growers pick the berries using clackety motorized machines.

The machines have a row of movable metal teeth in the front that comb the berries off the plants. A bucket conveyor carries the berries, along with some twigs and leaves, away from the metal teeth and dumps them into a burlap sack. When a sack is full, it is lifted off the machine. An empty sack is put in its place.

The sacks are emptied onto metal screens to separate the berries from their leaves and twigs. The berries fall through the screens into sturdy plastic crates. When the crates are three high, they are bundled together with a webbed nylon belt.

Now the cranberries are ready to be moved off the bog. A helicopter lifts them into the air and gently sets them onto a flatbed truck, which carries them to a nearby packing plant. By using helicopters, growers avoid crushing next year's crop of berries, which are already in bud.

Meanwhile, cranberries that will be used in juices and sauces are picked by a different method, called wet harvesting. First the bog is flooded with water from a nearby swamp or pond. In a few hours, the cranberries are completely covered by water.

17

Then workers drive fat-tired vehicles called water reels, or "eggbeaters," through the bog. The spinning reels on the machines loosen the berries from the plants. The berries float free to the water's surface.

The floating cranberries make beautiful patterns on the water. They must be removed to waiting trucks. But how?

Workers start by assembling a corral made of boards held together at the ends by canvas hinges. The workers encircle the cranberries with the corral and draw them to one end of the bog.

Then a worker places a pipe just beneath the surface of the water in the middle of the cranberries. The pipe leads to a pump onshore, which sucks the berries — along with stray twigs and leaves and a certain amount of water — into a metal box called a hopper.

The hopper separates everything. The leaves and twigs go into a truck, which later dumps them into a compost heap. The water goes back through a pipe into the bog. And the berries go into a trailer truck. The workers push the berries to the pipe opening until the truck is full to the brim with berries — 40,000 pounds' worth! These will go into cranberry sauces and cranberry juices.

At the packing plant, the cranberries that have been brought in to be packaged are sorted by a machine that bounces them. Fresh, firm berries bounce easily over the machine's inch-high "bounce boards." Bruised, rotten berries do not. Every cranberry gets four chances to clear a bounce board. The berries that clear the boards are carried away by conveyor belts for bagging. The berries that don't are discarded.

The berries that pass the bounce test are further checked for freshness by experienced workers. Then they are bagged by machines and boxed by hand for shipment to grocery stores everywhere. Cranberries grow in Massachusetts, New Jersey, Wisconsin, Washington, Oregon, and British Columbia. Except for Concord grapes and blueberries, they are our only native North American fruit.

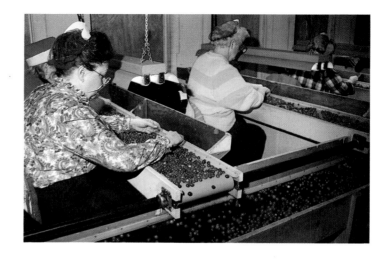

In December, growers flood their bogs with water to protect next year's fragile buds from the winter cold. By January, the top few inches of water are frozen solid. Come spring, though, the ice will melt, and the growers will pump the water away. The sun will shine. The rain will fall. In June, the cranberry bogs will blossom again.